Caged

The Club

Re

Copyright

CAGED

Cover by Aila Glass Designs

About This Book

She finally broke free of her past. There's no way she's going to allow herself to be trapped in a relationship again.

Janie spent way too many years denying her true desires and wasting her life on an emotionally abusive man. It was only when she started secretly coming to Club Surrender that she realized that even in submission she could be in control. Free and finally able to explore her bisexuality, the last thing she wants to do is fall in love again, even though the rope expert who ties her up is very appealing...

Skye is the newest dominatrix at Seattle's women only BDSM club. They call her "The Ice Queen" due to her cold and emotionless demeanor, something that has served her well in both her high-powered career and her dominatrix role. But after years of bad experiences at other clubs, she's finally found a home. She's also found something unexpected: her soul mate.

Skye wants to make Janie hers forever, but the younger woman doesn't believe in romance – and there's no way she's willing to commit to a new relationship so soon. With a little patience and some help from their friends, Skye devises a plan to win her submissive's heart.

Caged is book five in the *Club Surrender* instalove lesbian romance series. Each book is a fun and steamy standalone with matchmaking dommes, loving relationships, and a sweet happily ever after.

These books are intended for mature audiences.

Be sure to check out a free preview of Reba Bale's lesbian romance "The Divorcee's First Time" at the end of this book!

Dedication

To everyone who realizes that neurodivergence can be a superpower.

Join My Newsletter

Want a free book? Join my weekly newsletter and you'll receive a fun subscriber gift. I promise I will only email you when there are new releases, free books, or special sales you'll want to see.

Visit my newsletter sign-up page at bit.ly/RebaBaleSapphic[1] to join today.

1. https://bit.ly/RebaBaleSapphic

Janie

Club Surrender was jam packed tonight. I pushed my way through the crowd, looking for my friend Sarah. We'd made plans to watch the rope play demonstration while her fiancée, Marlena, tortured some subs.

When Sarah asked me to come with her to Club Surrender a few months ago, I was thrilled. I'd long had a fascination with BDSM, particularly spanking and bondage, but didn't feel comfortable going to a club by myself. The minute I walked into Club Surrender for the first time, it was like coming home.

It wasn't just that this was the first BDSM club in the country that catered only to self-identified women, although that was definitely a selling point. No, it was the sensation of being surrounded by people like me for the first time in my life. People who liked a little pain. People who craved submission. People who were kinky, but not violently so. It was completely freeing.

Tonight I came here with an extra spring in my step. I'd finally kicked my asshole boyfriend Jonathan to the curb. It was a long time coming. We'd dated for years and slowly, so gradually that I hadn't even noticed it, he'd become mean and controlling. I found myself sneaking around to the activities I liked, including coming here to Club Surrender, because Jonathan didn't approve of my doing anything but going to work and hanging out at home with him, being at his beck and call.

Jonathan was also emotionally abusive. He was continually criticizing me, insulting me, or gaslighting me in his effort to tear me down and make me and everyone around us think I was crazy.

He hated my relationship with Sarah and had tried to sabotage it multiple times, but fortunately our friendship had withstood everything he tried to do. Sarah hated Jonathan as much as he hated her, but she'd always been too nice to say anything.

I knew she worried though. I'd convinced myself that she was overreacting. Until the night that Jonathan insulted me one too many times. When I got angry and told him to stop insulting me, he punched me in the face, leaving me with a black eye and a healthy fear of what he'd do next. He'd apologized of course, and promised that he'd never do it again, but I wasn't going to wait around to see if it was true.

I took the day off work the next day and moved into Sarah's apartment. She spent all her time at her girlfriend Marlena's house anyway and was glad to have me sublease from her. Then I filed a police report, changed all my passwords, got a new phone number, and petitioned for a restraining order.

The domestic violence advocate who was assigned to me by the court helped me see that emotional and financial abuse was still abuse. She helped me create a plan for avoiding my ex and suggested checking my car and purse for tracking devices. I'd found two and flushed them both down the toilet. I'd had no idea that Jonathan's controlling behavior had gone so far.

The sad thing was that I didn't even love him. Sure, I thought I had a long time ago, but a combination of inertia and Jonathan convincing me that no one else would want me kept me under his control. Now that the blinders were off, I was pissed at myself for wasting so much time with that asshole.

I knew I hadn't seen the last of Jonathan, but I was finally taking steps to be independent, and I was pretty damned proud of myself for that. It would be a long time before I considered being in a relationship again, that's for sure.

"Hey, sweetie!" Sarah walked up to me and threw her arms around my shoulders, pulling me into a tight hug. "How are you doing?"

"Better now that I'm here," I said honestly.

Something about Club Surrender calmed my mind, even if I didn't do a scene. I just wished I could afford to come here more often.

Sarah and I walked around talking as we watched some of the public play scenes, and my eyes caught on a blond woman wearing high heels, a G string, and a tiny bikini top. Sarah's eyes followed my gaze.

"She's cute," Sarah said, her tone imbued with subtext.

I turned to frown at her. "What do you mean?"

"It's just, well, I know you've been with a man for a long time, but have you ever thought about being with a woman?"

"Are you trying to recruit me to the lesbians now, Sarah?" I teased. "Is there a quota you have to meet or something?"

I was deflecting. The truth was, I'd been attracted to women for a long time. I just didn't know what to do with that, especially when I was in a heterosexual relationship. I needed to spend some time working on myself before I even considered dating anyone, man or woman.

"I get a toaster oven if I convince you to join Team Lesbian," she replied, referencing an old joke about 'turning' women into lesbians.

"I'm not opposed to being with a woman," I admitted. "I've found myself, uh, a little bit attracted to a couple of the dommes when we were doing scenes. But I've never even kissed a woman."

"Not even in college?" Sarah seemed surprised.

"Nope. But I'm realizing that I'm attracted to more than one kind of person." My face flamed, even though there was nothing to be embarrassed about.

"Well, my budding bisexual, you're at the perfect place to experiment. And when you decide that you're ready to date, just let me know. Between me and Marlena, I'm sure we know someone who would be a good match for you."

I linked my arm with her and led her towards the stage as someone announced that the rope play demo was about to start.

"Do you get the toaster oven when I agree to a date? Or do I actually have to have sex first for it to count?"

"I'll have to check the bylaws and get back to you."

Skye

"Thanks for agreeing to do this," Angela said.

I gave her a nod. "It's no problem, rope play is one of my specialties and I love teaching it to other dominants."

The club owner gave me a smile. "Well, we're lucky to have you here, that's for sure."

Glancing around the crowded club, I had to appreciate Angela. She was a sharp businesswoman. A dominant herself, she'd gotten tired of the toxic masculinity that seemed to be present at a lot of BDSM clubs. I'd seen quite a bit of that myself at other clubs I'd visited, especially as a female dominant.

Angela decided to create a club where women, including trans women, could come and explore their kinky sides in a safe and nurturing atmosphere. Club Surrender had been a big hit right from the beginning.

I'd moved here a couple of months ago from Boston, and I'd been pleasantly surprised to find a club like this here in Seattle. I already felt comfortable here – or as comfortable as I did anywhere.

Being neurodivergent, I didn't always pick up on social cues. The unwritten rules of society confused me. It was part of what drew me to BDSM. The rules were clearly defined and agreed to ahead of time. As a dominant, the intense focus for detail that I had helped me immensely. I loved to create complex scenarios designed to bring my subs right to the edge.

"Are you looking for a play partner tonight?" Angela asked. "There are a lot to choose from. Your demonstration really drew a crowd."

My eyes scanned the packed room again. "I'll play it by ear."

A little while later it was time for my demonstration. I stood quietly at the side of the main stage as Angela introduced me. I smoothed my hand down my dress, a short off-the-shoulder number that was black and sparkly. The knit hugged my curves nicely and I'd noticed more than one admiring look as I'd walked on the stage. I'd worn my long blonde hair down around my shoulders, curled in soft waves.

I might not be the best looking woman here tonight, but I looked pretty good for forty-four.

I began my presentation, explaining the key elements of rope play while the audience listened with rapt attention.

My gaze caught on a woman near the front of the crowd. She was off to the side a bit, talking to a woman who I knew was with Marlena, one of the other dommes here. I only knew that because I'd seen them making out and overheard someone talking about how great it was that they'd finally gotten engaged.

The woman who caught my eye was short and curvy. She was young, and while in this light I couldn't get a good estimate of her age, I knew she had to be at least fifteen years younger than me.

She had brown hair that was pulled up in a high ponytail, with curly tendrils framing her heart-shaped face. Even from here I could see that the girl was beautiful. She had full, high breasts encased in a red corset, a narrow waist, and rounded hips that stretched the limits of black leggings.

As I stared at her, I felt something I hadn't felt in a very long time: desire. There was something more there too, it was almost like I was...drawn to her.

"I would like to have a volunteer please," I told the audience. "Someone who will be comfortable being tied up."

Several hands rose into the air. When I saw the curvy girl's hand pop up, I couldn't resist pointing at her.

"You. In the red corset. You may come up here."

She made her way to the stage excitedly. "Thank you, Mistress."

I nodded, but otherwise did not acknowledge her comment. In the other parts of my life, I'd learned that people thought my behavior was rude, but here in the club, it just added to my mystique as a dominatrix.

"We will start by learning one of the basic knots, called the Somerville Bowline. Our submissive will sit on this bench, and I will demonstrate."

I led the girl into place, then gently pulled her arms behind her. Several people crowded around as I carefully restrained her wrists, then demonstrated how the knot worked.

"It's very important to check in with your submissive as you go along to verify that the positioning of the body or the tightness of the rope are not causing discomfort."

I walked to the front of the girl's body and met her eyes, startled to realize that she was a little older than I'd first thought, maybe in her early thirties.

"Are you experiencing any significant discomfort?" I asked.

"No, Mistress."

"Get out the flogger and see if she changes her mind!" someone called from the audience.

The crowd laughed, but I didn't respond.

"Now I will demonstrate using rope to restrain the arms to the torso. This type of binding immobilizes the upper body and requires complete trust between the dominant and submissive."

I began to wrap the rope around the girl's body as I spoke, trying very hard not to get distracted as I worked. There was something about her that made me feel off balance. Every time I touched her, my blood seemed to warm. I was incredibly attracted to her, which was very unusual for me, but it felt like more than simple attraction.

"If your submissive is topless," I continued, trying hard to focus, "You can also tie the ropes in such a way as to cause reduced blood flow to the breasts, causing a similar reaction as nipple clamps, but much more diffuse."

A few minutes later I finished the simple rope corset, stretching the silk cords over her clothing, then binding her arms to her torso. I could have asked her to disrobe for a more authentic demonstration, but for some reason I didn't want all these women staring at my sub's naked body.

After demonstrating a couple of other knot techniques, I paused for questions, and then concluded the lesson. Angela hurried up to the stage to thank us both for participating, offering the girl a free pass for her role in the demonstration. She responded as if Angela had offered her a million dollars.

I took my time releasing her from my ties, somehow hesitant to let her go. Once the ropes were removed, the girl stood up and gave me a bright smile.

"Thank you, Mistress, that was a really cool experience. By the way, my name is Janie."

She reached out a hand, and I took it automatically. It proved to be a huge mistake, because the instant our skin touched, I felt a jolt of something electric that was so strong, I almost gasped. When I met her eyes, she looked a little dazed, telling me that she'd felt it too.

Suddenly she pulled away. "I, uh, I'd better go," she stammered. "Have a good night."

As she hurried off, for some reason I felt bereft.

Janie

"That rope demo the other night was cool," Sarah said over lunch a few days later. "I mean, I've had my hands and feet tied up before, but that was totally different. You couldn't move your upper body at all, and the knots made an interesting pattern."

"Yeah, it was pretty cool," I agreed.

If I closed my eyes, I could feel the light pressure of the rope tied around my body, the knots pressing against my clothing. I'd had my hands restrained a couple of times at the club as part of a scene, but I'd never actually been bound. Never felt so completely under another person's control. I would have thought that I'd hate that, and I probably would have with anyone else, but for some reason with Mistress Skye, I felt completely safe.

I'd had a dream about her the night after the demo. A sex dream. I'd woke up with my pulse hammering and my panties wet, only able to calm down once I'd slid my fingers in between my slipper folds and strummed my clit until I came.

"That Skye is quite beautiful," Sarah continued, oblivious to my inner turmoil.

"Yeah."

"She's got that calm, cold vibe about her. I can see why they call her the Ice Princess. I bet she she's hell on her team."

"Her team?"

"She's some kind of a high-powered scientist in the aerospace industry. A genius. Apparently, her current company had to pay a fortune to get her here from Boston."

I could see that. Intelligence had shone in her eyes, adding to her cold and standoffish demeanor.

"Hmm," I said, my tone deliberately non-committal.

I didn't fool my friend at all. "What? What's that face?"

I looked around furtively, then leaned across the table. "I had a very...physical reaction to her when I was on the stage. Like sexually, I mean. Then I had a naughty dream about her."

Sarah looked confused. "So?"

"That's never happened before," I explained.

"Never?"

"No, I don't usually have sex dreams. Besides, I've always thought I was straight."

I wasn't sure which of us I was trying to convince.

"You're not straight," Sarah said firmly. "I've seen you checking out women at the club, although maybe you weren't aware of it. Haven't you fantasized about any of the dommes you've scened? You said you'd felt some attraction there, are you telling me that you never got yourself off thinking about it later?"

"No."

Whatever glimmer of attraction that I felt in those scenes hadn't felt nearly as intense as the simple and impersonal over-the-clothes rope demonstration felt with Skye that night.

"Wow. Okay. Well, maybe you should try to get a scene with the rope lady and see where things go. You could see if she's attracted to you too."

"Most of the dommes at the club are strictly play partners, not sex partners," I reminded her.

"Yeah well, that hasn't stopped several of them from falling in love anyway." She held up her hand before I could respond. "I know, I know, you're never falling in love again. I'm just saying, Skye might be up for a little fun. Maybe she'll break your lesbian cherry for you."

Unsure how I felt about that, I changed the subject.

Later that same day I was working my second job as a waitress when I heard a familiar voice behind me.

"Janie? Is that you?"

I'd been daydreaming about Skye all day, so for a second, I thought I was hearing things. But sure enough, when I turned around, I saw the domme sitting at a table with another woman. For some reason, a rush of embarrassment and something that felt a lot like jealousy slammed into me.

"Oh hi." I lifted my order pad and looked between Skye and her companion, avoiding any direct eye contact. "What can I get you?"

"Another waitress, please."

Skye's words were clipped. It pissed me off. Was she so repulsed by me I couldn't even serve her a drink?

"I'm the only waitress on the floor right now, and I'm quite busy so either give me your order or quit taking up a table. Other customers are waiting to be seated."

Skye's eyebrows raised high on her forehead, and she almost looked impressed by my outburst.

"I'll have a bourbon please," she said finally. "Whatever is top shelf."

I resisted rolling my eyes, turning to her companion to get their order as well before heading back to the bar to turn it in. When I turned around, Skye was right behind me, her face blank but her eyes intense. I caught a whiff of her citrus shampoo.

"When will you be at the club again?" she asked. "I thought we might scene together."

For some reason, I had the impression that she was uncomfortable asking me but making herself do it anyway. I tamped down the thrill I felt at her invitation to play together.

"I won't be there any time soon," I said, stepping out from between her and the bar to give myself some space. My heart was racing, but I had no idea why. Did I have too much caffeine today?

"Why not?"

I stared at the floor, feeling my face heat, before I reminded myself that being poor wasn't a character flaw. I lifted my chin and met her eyes.

"The club is very expensive. I can only afford to visit when there's a special event or something."

There was a pause as she digested this information.

"You will visit me at the club Saturday night," she ordered. "I will leave you a guest pass so you can attend for no cost."

"Excuse me, you don't get to just order me around," I protested, fighting my instinct to go along with her.

I wanted to see her again. I wanted to see what it was like to submit to her. But I'd already been in a relationship with someone who wanted to control me. There was no way I wanted to start taking orders from anyone again.

"I hope that I'll see you Saturday," she stated softly. "I'd love to do a scene with you." She gave me another long inscrutable look before returning to her table.

I avoided her as much as possible until she and her companion finally left. When I went to clear the dishes from the table, I saw that Skye had left me a one hundred dollar bill as a tip along with a note that only said, *Seven p.m. Saturday.*

For some reason, it made me smile.

Skye

I was unaccountably nervous as I sat at the bar at Club Surrender, waiting to see if Janie would show up. When I saw her at the restaurant where she worked, I'd realized that I hadn't been imagining the strong pull I felt towards her. And when our eyes met, I realized with a start that I was in love with her.

It was ridiculous. People didn't fall in love at first sight, especially people like me. But I knew how I felt, and I wasn't one to shy away from hard things. I needed to make Janie mine, and I was hoping that playing together at the club would help with that, despite the way she'd practically ran away from me after the rope play demonstration.

It had never occurred to me that Janie – or anyone else – might find the club too expensive. I was a bit embarrassed at my privilege. Between a job that paid me very well, careful investments, and some family money that I'd inherited, I was quite well off. My financial advisor called me a millionaire. And while I lived simply, I'd certainly never had to worry about something like club admission.

Once we were together as a couple, I'd put Janie on my Club Surrender membership so she wouldn't have to worry about it, but for right now, I could purchase guest passes for her.

"Hey."

I was so deep in thought I didn't even hear Janie come up to me. She was dressed in a short black leather skirt, a tight white tank top that clung to her curves, and black Doc Martens. She looked adorable. I took a deep breath and reached for my domme persona.

"Is that how you greet me, girl?"

I saw the minute she mentally submitted to me. Her spine straightened but her eyes shifted to the floor. "My apologies. Good evening, Mistress."

"Good girl," I praised. "You may relax."

Her eyes lifted to mine, then skittered away.

"Are you ready to play? I have reserved a room and also reviewed your paperwork to assess your preferred activities."

As a dominatrix I was required to familiarize myself with my submissive's preferences, particularly their hard and soft limits.

"Yes, Mistress."

"Let's go."

I headed towards the hallway leading to the private rooms, confident that she would follow me. Sure enough, when I opened the door to room five, she was right behind me.

"You will undress completely," I ordered.

"Yes, Mistress."

Janie removed her tank first, then her bra, revealing heavy round breasts and a narrow waist. Her skirt and panties followed, then she kicked off her boots, leaving her standing totally naked. She gripped her elbows behind her back, her gaze downward as she waited for my instructions.

I was planning to tie her up. Of course, I was planning to tie her up. I loved doing it, that's why I'd studied rope play and gotten to be an expert on it. But first, communication was the most important thing in BDSM.

"I have reviewed your hard limits, and they are similar to mine. Is there anything else you want to communicate before we begin?"

"No, Mistress."

"Very well. We will use the stoplight system, red, green, yellow. Do you understand?"

"Yes, Mistress."

She was so sweetly submissive it made my heart ache. I led her to a straight back chair and directed her to sit forward on the seat with her feet on the floor and her hands on her knees, palms up. I pulled out a long length of jute rope that I'd selected just for today, the red color a nice contrast against Janie's pale skin.

Without a word I began wrapping the rope around her torso, the motion almost hypnotic to me. I did a little more elaborate corset design than I had in the demonstration, but not too much so, given she was new to this. Once she had more experience, I'd spend more time binding her into more complicated positions. In my mind's eye, I pictured Janie bound and hanging from the ceiling, totally at my mercy, and pressed my thighs together.

When I wrapped the rope around her breasts, I tightened it slightly to add a bit of pressure, squeezing the flesh. It immediately made her nipples harden. Janie was completely silent while I worked.

Once I'd finished the corset, I led her to a padded bench, briefly debating how I wanted her. Finally, I lowered her onto her back, bent her knees, and tied her wrists and ankles together with a short length of rope. This tie left her legs spread, her pussy completely exposed to my view.

I leaned forward and to my satisfaction I saw moisture glistening on her lower lips. My girl was already aroused just from being tied up.

"Are you experiencing any pain?" I asked. "You might feel discomfort from the binding, but I do not want you to feel any pain. At least not right now."

"No, Mistress, I don't feel any pain."

"Very well."

I walked over to the bag I'd brought in with me and found what I was looking for.

"Now we will begin."

Janie

I was laying on this padded table that reminded me of a massage table, arms and legs completely immobilized as the cool air of the room caressed my naked body. I'd had my hands tied before, but I'd never been this completely immobilized. I tugged on my hands, testing the knots, and they didn't budge. I was completely trapped.

I waited for the panic to come, but instead I felt excited. Possibly more excited than I'd felt in my life.

Right now, Skye could do whatever she wanted to me, and in this position, I'd be helpless to resist. That thought made a rush of arousal flood my pussy.

A buzzing sounded in the room as Skye returned to the bench with a rather large vibrator in her hand. Without a word, she began sliding it up and down my slit, teasing me until I was digging my heels into the cushioned surface and lifting my hips to meet her. I couldn't get too far though before the restraints pulled me back.

I yelped as she slid the vibrator into my channel. I was dripping wet, but it was also petty big, based in how much it was stretching my pussy. There was a shift, and then I felt Skye's fingers digging painfully into my thighs as her tongue started circling my clitoris.

I'd never had a woman go down on me before. With the other dommes I'd played with, I'd been clear that toys were okay but personal contact wasn't. I hadn't given Skye that same restriction and given how incredible it felt, I was not regretting that decision.

Skye's mouth on my pussy was everything I never knew was missing in my life. She sucked my clit into her mouth and between that and the vibrator that was still buzzing insistently inside me, I couldn't forestall my orgasm.

"Ahh!"

I cried out, unable to form words as all the blood in my body seemed to head to my pussy. My attention was laser focused on the sensation of Skye suckling my swollen bud. My heart was hammering in my chest and my breath coming in harsh pants as I succumbed to the pleasure.

Skye lifted her head as I started to come down, then carefully removed the vibe and turned it off. I figured that we were done, but I figured wrong.

She stepped away for a minute, then returned with a small flogger made entirely out of rope. It had a braided handle, with several strings of rope coming out of the handle, each tied with a tight knot on the end. For a moment, she held it up in my line of vision.

"Do you like it? I made it myself," she said proudly.

"Yes, Mistress."

First, she just ran it up and down my body, teasing me with it, then she moved between my legs and tapped it against the top of my pussy. Despite the fact that it was the lightest of taps, everything was still super sensitive from my orgasm. I cried out.

Skye ignored me, tapping the rope flogger down one inner thigh, down to the ankle and across my pussy before doing the same thing on the other side. Each tap of the flogger left a slight sting that quickly dissipated.

She moved the flogger up, tapping along the swell of my belly from side to side before making her way to my breasts. The sensation of the rope slapping lightly against the soft skin of my breasts was incredible. As she tapped across my nipples over and over again, I began whining, close to coming again from the sensation.

Without warning Skye moved back to the bottom of the table, untying my legs and stretching them out. I wiggled them from side to side as full circulation returned. The other rope was still wrapped around my wrists, and Skye pulled my arms up over my head, securing the rope to something under the table but leaving my legs free.

Then she returned to her methodical tapping across my body with the rope flogger, reversing the direction she'd gone on the way up. Her touch was still light, but harder than before. My entire body was vibrating from being teased with the rope.

"Please, Mistress," I finally gasped when I couldn't take it anymore.

I knew it was against the rules to talk first, unless I was going to safe word out, but I needed to come so bad. I just needed a little something more to push me over the edge.

Skye seemed to know what I needed, because she shoved one finger inside my channel, thrusting in and out. Then she rotated her arm and ground the heel of her hand down hard against my clit.

This time when I came, I screamed from the force of it, thrashing against the restraints on my arms. I'd come before, probably hundreds of times, yet no other person had played my body as well as Skye did. I wanted more. But not just more orgasms, more Skye.

A flood of emotion hit my brain. Holy shit, I liked her! Liked her, liked her. Just because I had never felt particularly attracted to a woman, that didn't mean I couldn't, right? After all, sexuality was a spectrum. It was like I'd just had my heterosexual blinders removed and discovered something new.

And when Skye lowered her head and pressed her lips against mine, I knew I'd also discovered something so much better.

Skye

As a rule, I didn't get too close to my submissives. I didn't lick their pussies or fuck them with my fingers. And I certainly didn't kiss them. But I couldn't help doing any of that with Janie. I wanted to kiss every inch of her body, following the path of the rope flogger that I'd crafted with my own two hands, then sit on her face and demand that she eat me out.

But technically we hadn't discussed any of this. It was that thought that finally had me pulling away from her. We were both breathing heavily, and Janie's lips were swollen from my rough kisses.

We stared at each other for a long moment before, with great effort, I pulled away. I untied Janie's hands, then removed the rope from her wrists. I moved slowly, gently stroking her skin with my fingers as I released the knots. I pulled her to seated, loathe to remove the rope corset and end the scene until I heard the discreet knock on the door letting us know that our time was almost up.

I glanced at my watch in shock. Usually I was very good at managing time, but the hour with Janie had flown by more quickly than I expected.

"How are you feeling?" I asked her.

"Like a puddle," she said dreamily.

I watched her carefully, trying to determine if she was just loopy from sex or if she'd dropped into subspace. Her eyes cleared as she looked around at everything except me. Definitely just loopy.

I grabbed a section of rope, pulling her closer to me with the corset.

"Next time we will have longer to play," I promised. "I will fuck you until you're begging for mercy, and if you are a good girl, I will allow you to eat my pussy."

I loved edging a sub. Edging Janie would be especially fun, given that I was emotionally invested in her pleasure.

"There's a next time, Mistress?" she asked teasingly.

I nodded. "Now that I've found you, I'm compelled to keep you forever. You're mine."

Her eyes widened in alarm, and immediately the mood between us shifted.

"Untie me. Please."

Her voice was insistent.

It took only a few flicks of my wrists to release her from the corset, and the instant I slid the last of the rope away from her body she jumped off the table and rushed towards her clothes. The domme in me noted with pleasure the faint marks on her skin from the rope while the woman in me frantically tried to figure out what I'd done wrong.

What cue had I missed? Normally I didn't mind that my brain worked differently than most people's but right now, I hated it.

"I've upset you," I noted. "I apologize."

Janie turned to me as she pulled her shirt over her head.

"No, it's fine," she lied. "I just need to go."

"But...you need aftercare..."

She shook her head vigorously. "I wasn't in subspace, I feel perfectly fine."

I strode over to her, grabbing her arm gently even while I added a commanding tone to my voice. "I must insist that you at least stay to drink some water so I can verify that for myself."

She sighed in exasperation. "Fine."

I didn't understand her change in mood. Mentally I reviewed the last few minutes, finding nothing in our conversation that would explain such a dramatic switch in her mood.

After making sure the room was in order, we walked to the bar. I slid onto the stool next to Janie, gesturing for the bartender to bring us two bottles of water.

"You want some cookies too, Janie?"

I didn't know this bartender who was smiling at my submissive, but apparently she knew Janie. I felt the most ridiculous stab of jealousy until I noticed the engagement ring on the bartender's finger. She was just being friendly, I thought in relief.

Janie was ignoring me, looking around at everything except for me as she nibbled on a cookie while I studied her carefully. It was a big change from the talkative woman I'd observed on our previous meetings.

"How are you feeling?" I asked, remembering my job as a dominant. "Do you have any lingering pain or light-headedness?"

"I'm fine," she said curtly.

She glanced pointedly at the watch on my wrist, even though the watch face was turned away from her. Something about her energy was frantic. She drained her water, then jumped off her bar stool.

"I have to go now." She glanced at me over her shoulder, her expression unreadable.

"Thank you for the free pass and for the session. I...it was good. Really good. I enjoyed it."

Her words were completely at odds with the expression on her face. I wished desperately that I knew what I was missing right now.

"Goodbye Mistress Skye."

I watched as she walked out of the club, feeling completely confused about what had happened. I was still staring at the door when Marlena, one of the other dominants, sat down next to me.

"Hey Skye. Were you playing with Janie tonight?" Marlena asked.

"Yes."

Marlena gestured for a bottle of water. "How did it go?"

I didn't know Marlena too well, but she seemed nice. She was a pleasure domme who was well liked here at the club. I'd heard that she held some kind of philanthropic role for the giving arm of a local software company.

"We had a good scene," I said carefully. "But I think I maybe pushed her too hard. She practically ran away from me and tried to get out of aftercare."

"Did you injure her?" she asked sharply. "Is she hurt?"

I reared back. "No, no, nothing like that. I...I kissed her."

Marlena relaxed. "Oh, okay. Do you like her?"

"It's more than like," I said honestly. "But I don't think she's interested in me."

"She's likely not going to be interested in anyone right now," Marlena told me. "She just got out of a bad relationship."

I turned to face her, eager to learn more about the woman who had captivated me. "How do you know that?"

"She's best friends with my girlfriend, Sarah. She was dating this guy for years who was a total asshole, and they just broke up a few weeks ago. In fact, she's staying at Sarah's old apartment now since Janie was living with the guy and didn't have anywhere else to go."

"Guy? I thought she was queer?"

She'd certainly kissed me like someone who was attracted to women, and I'd seen her staring at my ass that night we did the bondage demonstration.

"Sarah thinks she's bisexual, but we don't know for sure. I doubt Janie does either. She's definitely bi curious if nothing else."

Marlena paused. "It will likely be a long time before she's ready to date again though, after all she's been through."

I lowered my head to the bar, then wrapped my arms around my head for good measure, pressing my face against the smooth wood. The pressure grounded me, slowing my racing heart.

"Uh, you okay there, Skye?"

"I have no idea."

Janie

I lay completely still in Sarah's old bed, reliving every single minute of my time with Skye tonight. I'd never kissed a woman before and never had a woman touch my pussy. After tonight I had to admit I was somewhere on the bisexual spectrum for sure.

In retrospect, I'd been attracted to women for a long time, but had never admitted it to myself before. That didn't make it any less true.

I wasn't upset about it or anything, just surprised. I'd never remotely considered the idea that I wasn't one hundred percent heterosexual before. Even when Sarah teased me about checking out women in the club, I thought it was just that – a joke. Now that I knew the truth, it was making me reconsider everything I knew about myself and wonder why I'd been so clueless up until now.

My phone buzzed. I grabbed it off the nightstand, seeing that I had a text from Sarah.

Sarah: ***Hey, how was your scene tonight?***

Me: ***How did you know I had a scene tonight? Are you spying on me? LOL***

Sarah: ***Marlena saw you there hanging out with the bondage lady.***

Me: ***Yeah, Mistress Skye invited me to come to the club and do a scene with her. She left me a free guest pass.***

Sarah: ***Wow, that was nice. Did she tie you up?***

Me: ***Yeah.***

Sarah: ***How elaborate was it?***

Me: ***She did a more complicated corset thing, then tied my ankles and wrists together.***

Sarah: ***Your wrists touch your ankles??? How long are your arms?***

Me: ***She bent my knees and there was some rope between them, then used some kind of rope flogger on me that she made herself.***

Sarah: ***That sounds hot.***

Me: ***It was. She also got me off with a vibe.***

Sarah: ***And? Anything else?***

Me: ***She kissed me.***

Sarah: ***How was it?***

Me: ***Incredible.***

My phone rang about three seconds later. I didn't even need to look at the screen to know it was my best friend.

"I knew it!" Sarah crowed, not even bothering with a greeting. "I knew you weren't as straight as you pretended to be."

"Does it really matter?" I asked wearily. "It's not like it makes a difference."

"It makes a difference in that the entire time I've known you I've watched you mold yourself to be what the men in your life wanted. Seeing you embrace your true nature makes me happy."

"I don't know that there's anything to embrace."

"Except Skye," she chuckled.

I could practically see her wagging her eyebrows at me over the phone. I sighed with exaggerated patience.

"Fine you get the...what is it you get as a prize? A toaster oven?"

"Yep."

There was a pause before Sarah spoke again.

"Do you like Skye?"

I sighed. "Yeah. I guess but..."

"But what?" my best friend asked.

"I like her more than I should, I guess. I mean, I'm still getting over Dickhead."

We'd made a pact to never mention my ex-boyfriend's name again.

"I shouldn't go falling in love with the first woman I kiss, right?" I clapped my hand over my mouth, hoping that Sarah wouldn't pick up on my use of the L word.

"Marlena said you practically ran out of Club Surrender," she asked instead. "Did something else happen? Are you okay?"

"Skye said something about keeping me forever and used the word 'mine'. I don't know, maybe she was just messing with me, but it freaked me out. I panicked."

"I don't think she was messing with you," Sarah said. "The Ice Queen is very literal, she's not one for flowery language or nuance, at least as far as I've seen."

Sarah spent way more time hanging around Club Surrender than I did now that she had a girlfriend there. She'd even purchased a monthly membership.

We'd run into Marlena the very first time we went to the club on Newbies Night. The curvy dominatrix was Sarah's brother's ex-girlfriend, but that didn't stop them from falling in love. They'd been together ever since.

When I didn't respond, Sarah added, "Skye was asking Marlena about you after you left. She even asked for your address. She said she wanted to come over and check on you."

I sat straight up, looking around the darkened room as if Skye were waiting to jump out from the shadows.

"Marlena told her she couldn't divulge your personal information without your permission, but that we'd check on you and let you know that Skye wanted to see you again."

I breathed a sigh of relief. Or maybe it was disappointment. "Oh. Okay. Thanks for passing on the message."

"Are you going to see her again?" Sarah asked curiously.

"I don't know."

"Well, you're bound to run into her at the club, right?"

"If I go back again."

As if I could stay away...

Skye

When an entire week went by without seeing or hearing anything about Janie, I decided that it was time to track her down. I wasn't going to be a stalker or anything, I just wanted to talk to her again. I needed to make sure that she was okay.

After work one night I decided to go to the bar that I'd seen her working at when I'd gone out with a coworker for drinks. It was a Wednesday, the same day I'd been there before, and I was hoping that she had a set schedule there. I got stuck in the lab at work a bit longer than I wanted though, and when I got to the bar, I didn't see her anywhere.

"Is Janie working tonight?" I asked another waitress.

"Yeah, but she's on break right now. What do you want with her?" The woman gave me a hard look, like maybe she thought I was there to serve a subpoena.

"I'm a...friend."

"Oh, well in that case then, I think she's probably out in the back courtyard. It's through that door." She pointed to a short hallway.

"Thanks."

It was a warm, dry night, unusual for this time of year in Seattle, and I could see why Janie wanted to take her break outside. I walked out the back door of the bar, which opened into a courtyard where I knew they had bands perform on weekends in the summer. Janie was sitting at a picnic table at the far end, eating a sandwich and reading something on a tablet in the fading light.

"Hi Janie."

She startled at my voice.

"Oh my God, I was so engrossed in my book I didn't even hear you coming," she said ruefully. "What are you doing here, Skye?"

"Looking for you." I gestured at the table. "Is it okay if I join you for a few minutes?"

"Okay."

She looked at me expectantly as I mentally pulled up the prepared words I'd memorized.

"I want to apologize to you for our scene last week. I realize that something I did upset you, and I want to assure you that was not my intention."

I still wasn't quite sure what exactly that was, but I'd learned long ago it was easier to apologize anyway.

Janie gave me a soft look. "You don't need to apologize. It wasn't you, it was me. I freaked out."

"Why?"

She looked around, a slight pink flush rising on her cheeks.

"I've never kissed a woman before," she said.

"You didn't like it?" I asked, trying to not look surprised at her admission.

That had been the best kiss of my life. I was going to be extremely disappointed if she told me that she'd hated it.

"No, I uh, I liked it. It's just that, besides the fact that I've never kissed a woman, I've never had a woman go down on me or...you know, use their hand on me like that and it just, well, it created a lot of confusing emotions for me."

"I didn't realize any of that."

"How could you?" she asked.

"It's more than that though, isn't it?" I pressed. "We were joking about if we'd have another play session, and that's when you became upset."

"You said you wanted to keep me forever, and you said I was yours," she reminded me. "It felt like too much, too soon. But then later I thought, maybe you were just kidding, and I overreacted, and then I felt embarrassed."

I reached across the table and took her hand in mine.

"I wasn't kidding. I'm pretty much never kidding about anything," I confessed. "But I'm sorry that it felt like I was pushing you, Janie. I'm not very good at the rules of social interaction. I tend to say whatever is on my mind, but I know it can throw people off."

She squeezed my hand, and I let out the breath I was holding.

"It's okay, it's just that the last person who was talking about spending forever with me in the beginning of a relationship turned out to be a controlling asshole who tried to isolate me from my friends and family," I explained. "I took a lot of crap from him for way too many years and when we broke up, I promised myself I wouldn't let myself be controlled like that again."

Even though I normally struggled to pick out subtext, I was pretty sure I was reading the subtext of this conversation loud and clear.

"Did he hurt you?" I asked, my voice deceptively calm despite the anger building inside me.

Janie pulled her hand away, almost shrinking into herself.

"He was mostly emotionally abusive," she said quietly. "Insulting me. Tearing me down. Making me think that I was the crazy one. Until the night I finally defended myself and spoke back to him. I don't know what my issue was that I allowed it to go on for so long, but let's just say that being punched in the face was the final straw for me. The first time he hit me, that's when I left."

I'd never felt true rage before that moment. Whoever this man was who'd abused Janie, I wanted him to suffer.

"What's his name?" I asked.

She frowned. "What? Why does it matter?"

"I will ruin him," I vowed.

I was going to hire a private detective and dig up all the dirt I could on this guy. I had no doubt that a guy like that had a lot of dirt to dig up, and when I found it, I'd make him regret the day he ever hurt my woman.

"It's none of your business," Janie said firmly, the wall back up between us.

She gathered up the rest of her lunch and her tablet and stepped away from the table.

"I have to get back to work. See you around."

Janie

The next few weeks passed quickly. I was still working two jobs, trying to dig myself out of the financial hole that leaving my ex had created. At some point Jonathon convinced me that we should have a joint bank account for household and shared expenses, and when I left him after he hit me, the first thing he did was drain all the money out of that account.

When I went to the bank, they told me that there was nothing they could do, a joint account meant that he had equal access to the money. Since I'd been putting my entire paycheck into the joint account, I was left with the couple hundred dollars I had in my individual savings account.

I was such an idiot. I'd heard the advice that women should always have their own money in case of an emergency, but I hadn't listened.

Sarah had offered to let me stay in her apartment for free until I got back on my feet, but there was no way I was going to take advantage of my friend like that. I insisted on subletting. I had a sneaking suspicion that she was undercharging me for the rent, but I didn't want to look at that too closely. Not right now when I had a car payment, student loan payments, and a bunch of credit cards I needed to pay.

Unfortunately, even with working two jobs, I had zero cash left to do anything fun, like go to Club Surrender.

Jonathan would have never understood my going to a place like that, so I'd lied and told him that I was going to a book club meeting whenever I went to the club. I'd only been there twice since the break-up. I'd already purchased a ticket for the rope demo before I left Jonathan, and then I got that pass from Skye the second time.

Right now, I couldn't afford to waste a single dollar on anything that didn't help me get out of the financial mess I was in.

When I came back into the bar after we talked at the picnic table, Skye was seated at a table in my section. I thought she'd try to talk to me some more, but instead she acted like I was any other waitress, other than the way her eyes followed my every move. She ordered a Manhattan and a basket of fries, lingered over them for a while, then took off, leaving me a one hundred dollar bill as a tip.

Over the next few weeks we went through the same routine. Skye came every Wednesday night after work, sat at the same table, ordered the same drink and fries, then left me a crisp one hundred dollar bill as a tip.

Other than small talk, we didn't say too much. She didn't ask me any personal questions or suggest we get together. Often, I was the only waitress on the floor and didn't have time to talk. But I felt her eyes on me, watching me carefully. It should have been creepy, but in actuality it felt kind of comforting, like she was watching out for me.

One Wednesday, about a month after the picnic table conversation I was coming out of my day job at a marketing company when I heard someone call my name. My ex-boyfriend Jonathan was leaning against the building, looking more haggard than I'd ever seen him. Normally he was well dressed, clean shaven, without a hair out of place. Today he was wearing ratty old jeans and sporting at least a few days' worth of scruff on his chin, his eyes ringed by dark circles.

I tamped down the ingrained urge to take care of him.

"Janie."

"What are you doing here Jonathan? I would have thought the restraining order would have made it clear that I didn't want you anywhere near me."

He stepped closer, and I held up my hand. "Don't think I won't call the cops on you, because I will."

"I need you to call off your people," he said aggressively, although his eyes looked a little wild.

"What are you talking about?"

"C'mon Janie. My car gets repossessed, I get fired from my job for being a liability after someone sends them a copy of the restraining order and dozens of texts between us, the County comes to the house and seizes my cat saying I don't have a license, my cell phone is forwarded to a sex chat line, and now I have a computer virus which ruined my hard drive and emptied my bank account. I get it. You're angry with me, but enough is enough."

I frowned in confusion. "You've made a lot of enemies I'm sure, maybe it was one of them."

"I know that was you. It had to be." He glared at me like he wished he could incinerate me with his eyes. "Look, I'm sorry you made me so mad that I hit you one damned time, but you don't have to ruin my life over it."

That was textbook Jonathan. The problem always was that I'd done something to make him behave a certain way, he never took responsibility for anything. I felt a surge of anger at both of us. Him for being such an asshole, and myself for putting up with it.

"To be clear, you did way more than hit me," I said firmly.

Jonathan's fingers were twitching like he was dying to come at me, but with the crowd of people walking by on the sidewalk, he didn't dare do it.

"Whatever is happening now, you can blame karma, not me. I've moved on, and I suggest you do the same."

He shoved a shaking finger in my face and growled in a menacing voice. "Call. Off. Your. Dogs."

When my ex-boyfriend stormed off, I sat on one of the steps leading up to my office and took several deep breaths. What was Jonathan going on about? I hadn't shared the restraining order with anyone, although those kind of things were easy to get copies of since they were public record.

But tapping into phone records and creating elaborate viruses, that seemed like it would take a criminal mind. Or someone who had the money to fund a criminal mind. A vision of those hundred dollar bills that Skye left for me every week flashed through my mind. I remembered Sarah saying something about how Skye had an important job, although I couldn't remember exactly what it was.

"I will ruin him." Skye's words a few weeks ago played on repeat in my head.

Surely it wasn't her? There was only one way to find out...

Skye hadn't even sat down at her usual table that night before I strode over and grabbed her wrist.

"Gina! I'm taking my break now!" I called to the woman behind the bar as I tugged Skye through the bar and out to the courtyard.

As soon as we were alone, I rounded on her. "By any chance have you been fucking with my ex-boyfriend?"

Her eyes bounced between mine. "How mad will you be if I say yes?"

Skye

"Out with it, Skye. Tell me everything."

I'd never seen this bossy side of Janie, it was kind of cute. Not that I would tell her that. I wasn't a total idiot.

"Did you get Jonathan fired, get his truck repossessed, his cat taken away, and his bank account drained?"

My investigator had been busy. It sounded like he'd made good progress.

"I am unable to do any of those things," I answered carefully. "I'm a researcher."

Janie took a deep breath. "You're rich, aren't you?"

I frowned at her change in subject. "I am comfortably wealthy, yes."

"Did you hire someone to mess with Jonathan?" she asked.

"Oh. Yes. I did do that."

There was no sense in lying. Clearly Janie had figured out I was behind her ex-boyfriend's string of bad luck, and even if I didn't suck at subterfuge, I didn't want to lie to her. She was too important to me.

"What else do you have planned?" She seemed more curious than angry right now.

"I require plausible deniability," I told her, which was exactly what I'd told the firm that I'd hired to dig up dirt on the asshole who'd hurt my woman. As I suspected, there was a lot of it. I'd left it to the firm's discretion how to handle things, and I had to admit, I was impressed with their thoroughness.

"You said you would ruin him, and you did," she mused, almost as if she was talking to herself. "I can't believe you did that."

I opened my mouth to ask how angry she was, but she grabbed my shoulders, whipped me around, and slammed my body into the brick wall that was now behind me. Before I processed what was happening, Janie crowded up against me, took my cheeks in her hands, and pressed her lips against mine. Her kiss was rough and claiming and everything in my body thrilled at the sensation.

My arms snaked around her waist, pulling her even closer to me as she ground her body against mine. I relaxed against the wall, happy to let Janie take the lead. Our tongues tangled as we dry humped each other against the wall, every part of me humming with excitement.

A door opened somewhere else in the courtyard, and we pulled apart, breathing heavily.

Janie looked up at me, her face soft.

"I can't condone what you did," she said quietly. "But I have to admit it feels good to have someone in my corner for a change."

Everything inside me breathed a sigh of relief.

"I'll be in your corner forever," I told her. "I like you Janie, more than I've liked anyone before. But I understand that you're coming out of a bad relationship and haven't had experience dating women, so we'll go slow. If you'll just agree to give me a chance?"

I'd gone after Janie's ex because I cared about her, not because I wanted to manipulate her into dating me. I wanted to be clear the choice was hers. She'd already been in a relationship where someone had taken away her power.

Janie didn't hesitate. "I'll give you a chance, Skye, but I can't make any promises about the future."

"Understood. How about we spend some time getting to know each other? I have to go out of town tomorrow for a family thing, but I'll be back next Thursday. Maybe we could...text?"

"Texting sounds good," she said, pulling out her phone. "What's your number?"

After she'd keyed in my number, I decided to be bold. "How about you come to the club with me next Friday after I get back, then we could have dinner somewhere after our scene, if that works for you?"

I couldn't quite interpret her expression, but I felt a profound sense of relief when she nodded.

"Next Friday is good."

"Great, I'll leave you a guest pass."

Janie

Skye and I spent the next week texting whenever one of us was free. We asked each other dozens of questions, trying to get to know each other better, and sharing snippets from our lives. I'd even started sending her funny memes, and while her response was generally a rolling eyes emoji, I knew instinctively that she was enjoying them.

I dressed carefully for my date with Skye on the following Friday. Knowing that we were going out to dinner after our play session, I decided to wear a dress with super sexy underwear beneath. The dress was a simple black sheath that I'd paired with a short jacket and knee high boots. It was perfect for a night out.

Skye was sitting at the bar when I arrived, talking to Marlena and another dominatrix named Lauren who was a fixture at the club. Skye and Marlena were talking while Lauren was flirting with her wife Kristina, who was working behind the bar tonight.

"Hey all," I greeted.

My eyes met Skye's. "Good evening, Mistress Skye."

Despite my deferential greeting, I couldn't help the grin that split my face. I was happy to see her again. Our week of texting had given me a level of ease with her that I hadn't had before.

"Janie," Skye said in the icy voice she almost always used. "You will follow me."

I followed her order without hesitation, following her down the hallway.

Like me, Skye was wearing a simple black dress, although hers was sparkly and hung off her shoulders. The fabric clung to her lean but curvy body, ending mid-thigh. Black stilettos added several inches to her height.

We were in room eight today, and as soon as she closed the door, Skye pulled me in for a long, hard kiss. Then she took a deep breath, putting on her domme persona, and stepped back.

"Undress," she ordered. "Take everything off."

Knowing she was watching, I undressed slowly, gradually revealing my new underwear. The bra had snug cups, with a series of criss crossing straps down my ribcage and over my shoulders. The panties were similarly constructed, with a solid crotch connected to straps that ran across my ass and hip bones. They were a little uncomfortable and totally a bitch to put on, but they were sexy as hell.

I knew Skye agreed when she ordered, "Keep those on."

That was good. There'd be nothing sexy about me getting out of this complicated underwear. She might have to cut me out of it. I removed my boots, then waited for further instruction. Skye walked around me slowly, not saying a word.

"I hardly know where to start," she whispered to herself.

After a few more moments of hesitation, she led me to a padded spanking bench. I immediately felt relaxed.

During my very first visit here at Club Surrender I'd done a scene with Mistress Zelda. She'd paddled my ass until I was sobbing in relief. There'd been absolutely nothing sexual about what she did, but it had been exactly what I needed at the time. Every spanking session since then had brought me that exact same sense of peace. Now whenever I had a bad day, I craved the relief of a good spanking.

Bending at the waist, I lowered my upper body onto the bench, bringing my knees to rest onto the lower section. I felt the slide of soft rope as Skye tied my calves to the bottom section of the bench, then moved around and tied my wrists to the other side. I tested the restraints, finding myself immobilized.

"Do you feel any pain? Any pinching?" she asked.

"No, Mistress."

She brought her hand down on my fabric-covered ass hard. "You will soon."

Thwack!

Skye gave me three or four more smacks with her hand before walking away for a moment.

"We need something sturdier than my hand if I want you to feel it through those panties," she said.

I heard a hiss of air right before a paddle came down, hard enough that I gasped.

Thwack!

Skye started paddling me at a steady pace, her strokes firm, even, and as perfectly timed as a metronome. Even with the protection of my panties, heat bloomed across my ass cheeks, each smack of the paddle leaving a sting that took an increasingly long time to dissipate.

I felt the tears coming, and momentarily struggled against my restraints as my mind and body resisted submission. Skye came down particularly hard right where my ass met my legs.

"Be still!" she ordered. "Relax your mind and give into the pain."

I started crying then, big gulping sobs that echoed in the room. A stream of tears slid down my cheeks and onto the floor beneath me, cleansing my soul and melting away all the stress of the last several weeks. Skye stopped every few minutes, moving around to study my face and ask me if I was using my safe word.

Each time I answered, "No, Mistress."

This. This was why I kept coming to Club Surrender long before I met Skye. Spanking was like therapy to me, breaking me down and leaving me stronger than before.

The methodical spanking gradually cleared my mind, bringing a sense of complete calm as all my attention focused on the spanking. When I heard Skye drop the paddle to the floor with a soft thud, I almost asked her to keep going.

Skye knelt in front of the bench, and to my surprise, she pushed down the top of her dress and unclasped the front closure of her strapless bra. She was twelve years older than me, but Skye's breasts were still firm and perky in a way I knew mine would never maintain. She pressed a nipple against my lips, and I dutifully opened, sucking in as much of her breast as I could. Without prompting, I began circling her nipple with my tongue.

I was dying to pull her closer, to touch her, but with my hands and legs still immobilized, all I could do was let her use my mouth.

"Suck harder," she ordered.

I realized it was the first time I'd had a woman's breast in my mouth. Drawing on what I liked, I sucked and licked and teased her breast between my teeth until her nipple was a hard point in my mouth. Then she shifted, and I gave the same attention to the other breast.

It was surprisingly arousing, leaving my own nipples hard and my panties sodden.

"You've never sucked a woman's tits before?" Skye confirmed as she pulled out of my mouth.

"No, Mistress." I licked my lips, wanting more.

"You're good at this," Skye said in a tone that told me she was very pleased at this development. "I'm going to make you come to show my appreciation."

I lifted my head so I could meet her eyes. "Maybe we can both come, Mistress."

"I won't punish you for talking out of turn because I like your suggestion," she said, a twinkle in her eyes. "Let's do it."

Skye

I made quick work of untying Janie before shoving off my skirt and underwear. I could see Janie watching me out of the corner of her eye, but she remained on the bench waiting for my instruction. Such a good little sub.

"You may get up," I told her, reaching out a hand to assist her.

The minute she was standing, her hot gaze traveled the length of my body down to the floor and back up again. I don't think she intended to do it, but she licked her lips hungrily.

I was quite a bit older than her, but between good genetics and a strict exercise routine, I knew I still looked good. But it was nice to see that Janie agreed.

Grabbing her wrist, I brought her to a chaise lounge in the corner. Or maybe it was a fainting couch, I wasn't sure. It was covered in vinyl, but I grabbed a sheet from a cabinet and tucked it into the cushions to give us a softer place to land.

"Lay down." At some point my voice had softened. I wasn't a dominant right now, I was a lover.

Janie complied, draping her curvy body over the sheet like she was in a photo shoot. I was obsessed with the intricate panties and bra she was wearing. They were sexy as hell, almost hotter than having her naked. Which gave me an idea.

"How about we make a bet?" I said.

Janie looked surprised at my change in topic. "What kind of bet?"

"If I can make you come without taking off your underwear, you'll agree to date me."

A range of emotions seemed to flash across her face, chief among them interest and fear. No worry, I was a patient person.

Janie affected a cocky tone. "You think you can make me come like that? Really? These are pretty thick panties."

"I don't *think* I can make you come, I *know* I can."

She raised one eyebrow. "Let's see what you can do then, Mistress."

Without a word, I strode forward and pushed her legs apart. Gripping the crotch of her panties, I pulled it away from her pussy, used my fingers to spread her pussy lips apart, then roughly shoved the fabric of the crotch inside her seam.

Janie gasped in surprise, her pupils wide with excitement.

"Bend your knees," I ordered.

The movement tilted her pelvis. Gripping either side of her underwear, I began sliding the fabric back and forth in her channel. The tightness of the fabric limited the range of motion, but it was enough to give her some rough friction that made her breath speed up.

When I was dying for some friction of my own, I pushed her legs straight and lowered myself on top of her, her thigh between mine, my upper body braced on my forearms. Leaning down, I kissed Janie deeply as I started to grind against her. I dug my toes in the fabric of the chaise as I slid up and down her body, getting myself off on her thigh while my own leg twisted to rub against the fabric covering Janie's clit.

My girl rolled her pelvis, sliding up to meet my thigh as we ground against each other. I was getting close fast, probably because I'd wanted this woman for what felt like forever. I changed positions slightly, adding more of my weight on top of her, and shifted my hand until I was cupping her throat. Her eyes widened as I gave her a little squeeze, just enough to let her know who was in charge.

"Fuck!" she gasped, and then Janie was shuddering beneath me, riding the waves of her pleasure, and rubbing her pussy harder against my thigh. I ground down on her, giving her all my weight and pressing my bare pussy against Janie's thigh so hard I half expected her to slip inside me.

I felt a jolt run down my spine, then my breath was catching in my throat as my orgasm hit me hard, making me shake and cry out as I came all over her leg.

"Janie!"

I could feel my wetness between our flesh as I ground and shuddered and panted through my own release. We continued rubbing our legs and pussies against each other, prolonging our pleasure.

We were both still recovering from our intense orgasms when we heard the knock on the door telling us that our time in the room was just about done.

Reluctantly I levered up to my hands and knees, hovering over Janie and staring at her until she met my eyes.

"I win," I whispered, giving her a smile. "I made you come without taking off your panties."

"Hopefully we both win," she replied, much to my surprise.

I pushed up to my knees, slipped off the chaise, and reached for her hand. "How about we have that dinner now?"

"I'm going to need you to be patient with me," she said, staring at the floor. "Let's have dinner and see how things go. We'll go from there."

"There's no rush, Janie. We have our whole lives to love each other."

Her eyes shot up to mine, her gaze searching. "Love?"

I nodded. I knew how I felt, but I was pretty sure that Janie felt the same. I could see it in her eyes even if she wasn't ready to admit it.

"I fell for you the minute I laid eyes on you," I said honestly. "And if you haven't figured it out already, I'm not a person who is super emotional. That's how I knew my feelings for you were real. But you're also going to need to be patient with me."

"How so?"

"I'll say the wrong thing. Miss social cues. Get so wrapped up in my work that I forget to come home for dinner. And...well, most people think I'm cold and insensitive. Rude even, although I don't intend to be."

Janie slid her hands around my neck, looking into my eyes for a long moment.

"There was nothing cold about you when you were grinding your pussy against my thigh," she said, giving me a warm look. "And if you miss something or say the wrong thing, I'll tell you. How about that?"

"What if I forget to come home for dinner?"

"I'll have to spank you, I guess."

I laughed.

"Hey! I'm supposed to be the dominatrix here," I reminded her with a smile.

"How about you just be my girlfriend instead?" she asked.

"That I can do."

Epilogue – Janie

Six months later...

"Come on, old lady, we're going to be late."

Skye hurried up, giving me a smack on the ass as she walked by. "Who are you calling an old lady?"

"Well, you are turning forty-five," I reminded her. "That's practically ancient compared to me."

"I'm only twelve years older than you," she protested.

When we first started dating, Skye was a little concerned that the difference in our ages would be a problem as we got older, but now that we'd been dating for just over six months, she seemed less bothered by it.

I certainly was. We might have an age gap, but we were perfectly matched. My relationship with Skye was the best I'd ever had – respectful, loving, and fun. I liked to think that I'd softened her up a bit, and Skye had definitely taught me that I could have a relationship free of hostility and negativity.

We hadn't had even one major argument in all these months together, although there was one thing that we didn't see eye-to-eye about: living together. Skye had been trying to get me to move in with her ever since about two weeks into our relationship, and I'd finally told her she couldn't ask me again for at least a year. I didn't want to rush into anything.

"I'll let you know when I'm ready to talk about taking the next step," I told her several months ago. "If you keep asking about it, it just makes me feel trapped."

"I would never trap you," she'd said. "I just want to wake up every day with the woman I love."

"I love you too, Skye, but I need time."

I was pretty sure she thought I'd never be ready, but after six months of therapy and six months in a good relationship, I was about as ready as I'd ever be. But she'd been patient, so I wanted to give her a grand gesture.

"We have reservations at *Novela*," I told her as we headed out the door. "I ordered us an Uber in case we want to drink."

The ride share was pulling up as we stepped outside. We were both quiet on the ride to the restaurant, and even after we were seated at our table, she remained silent. I glanced at my girlfriend a few times but couldn't get a bead on what she was thinking. Finally, I decided to ask. We'd promised each other not to have secrets.

"What are you thinking?" I asked. "I know you can't be concentrating on the menu that hard."

She put the menu on the table and grimaced.

"It's stupid, but I was thinking I'm going to be fifty in five years. I still feel like I'm in my twenties."

I knew she was in perimenopause now, and it was freaking her out a little. I wondered if she was having regrets.

"Are you sad that you didn't have kids?" I asked.

She shook her head immediately.

"I never wanted kids, and while I would have sucked it up if you really wanted them, I'm glad I don't have to." She paused, sending me a searching look. "You haven't changed your mind, have you?"

"No," I said emphatically. "Not about having kids anyway. However, I have changed my mind about something else."

"Can I get you ladies a drink?" The waiter chose that moment to approach our table.

"A bottle of merlot, please," I said firmly, without sparing him a glance.

I kept my gaze fixed on Skye as he scurried away. Reaching into my pocket, I pulled out a blue velvet box and slid it across the table. Her eyes widened as she realized what it was.

"I changed my mind about needing a year to make a commitment," I told her. "I'm ready now. I love you Skye, and I want us to get married."

Her jaw dropped, looking from me to the ring box and back to me. "You mean it? Do you really want to get married?"

"Yeah, I do."

She opened the box, pulling out the simple engagement ring I'd purchased for her. I'd kept working at the bar even after I paid off my bills so I could save up for a ring. It wasn't much, especially for a wealthy woman like Skye, but then again, she wasn't one for the trappings of money. My girlfriend lived simply.

She stared at the ring like it was worth a million dollars.

Anyone watching would think that her face was totally blank right now, but I'd learned to read her expressions over the time we'd been dating, and I could see that she was thrilled. Her eyes were glimmering with happiness and excitement.

"Put it on," I said.

The small diamond sparkled in the light as she slid the ring on her finger, then held it up for us to both admire.

"It fits perfectly," she said quietly.

"We fit perfectly. So, are you going to marry me or what?" I teased. "You didn't really answer me."

"Oh yeah, I'm totally going to marry you," she vowed. "As soon as possible."

She gave me a smile that lit up her whole face and I gave her a happy smile of my own in return. We both jumped out of our seats, meeting in the middle to share a long kiss. When we pulled back, everyone around us was clapping, obviously figuring out what was going on.

"We're getting married!" I said happily.

"Yeah, we are!"

"I love you, Skye" I whispered against her lips.

"I love you too. I can't wait to spend the rest of my life with you."

***

You can find more of Reba's lesbian romances at

Books2read.com/rl/lesbianromance[1]

If you liked this book, please consider leaving a review or rating to let me know.

Be sure to join my newsletter for more great books. You'll receive a free book when you join my newsletter. Subscribers are the first to hear about all of my new releases and sales. Visit my mailing list sign-up at bit.ly/RebaBaleSapphic[2] to download your free book today.

1. *https://books2read.com/rl/lesbianromance*

2. https://bit.ly/RebaBaleSapphic

Special Preview

The Divorcee's First Time
A Contemporary Lesbian Romance
By Reba Bale

"It's done," I said triumphantly. "My divorce is final."

My best friend Susan paused in the process of sliding into the restaurant booth, her sharply manicured eyebrows raising almost to her hairline. "Dickhead finally signed the papers?" she asked, her tone hopeful.

I nodded as Susan settled into the seat across from me. "The judge signed off on it today. Apparently his barely legal girlfriend is knocked up, and she wants to get a ring on her finger before the big event." I explained with a touch of irony in my voice. "The child bride finally got it done for me."

Susan smiled and nodded. "Well congratulations and good riddance. Let's order some wine."

We were most of the way through our second bottle when the conversation turned back to my ex. "I wonder if Dickhead and his Child Bride will last for the long haul," Susan mused.

I shook my head and blew a chunk of hair away from my mouth.

"I doubt it," I told her. "Someday she's gonna roll over and think, there's got to be something better out there than a self-absorbed man child who doesn't know a clitoris from a doorknob."

Susan laughed, sputtering her wine. I eyed her across the table. Although she was ten years older than me, we had been best friends for the last five years. We worked together at the accounting firm. She had been my trainer when I first came there, fresh out of school with my degree. We bonded over work, but soon realized that we were kindred spirits.

Susan was rapidly approaching forty but could easily pass for my age. Her hair was black and shiny, hinting at her Puerto Rican heritage, with blunt bangs and blond highlights that she paid a fortune for. Her face was clear and unlined, with large brown eyes and cheek bones that could cut glass. She was an avid runner and worked hard to maintain a slim physique since the women in her family ran towards the chunkier side.

I was almost her complete opposite. Blonde curls to her straight dark hair, blue eyes instead of brown, curvy where she was lean, introverted to her extrovert.

But somehow, we clicked. We were closer than sisters. Honestly, I don't know how I would have gotten through the last year without her. She had been the first one I called when my marriage fell apart, and she had supported me throughout the whole process.

It had been a big shock when I came home early one day and found my husband getting a blow job in the middle of our living room. It had been even more shocking when I saw the fresh young face at the other end of that blow job.

"What the fuck are you doing?" I had screeched, startling them both out of their sex stupor. "You're getting blow jobs from children now?"

The girl had looked up from her knees with eyes glowing in righteous indignation. "I'm not a child, I'm nineteen," she had informed me proudly. "I'm glad you finally found out. I give him what you don't, and he loves me."

I looked into the familiar eyes of my husband and saw the panic and confusion there. I made it easy for him. "Get out," I told him firmly, my voice leaving no room for argument. "Take your teenage girlfriend and get the fuck out. We're getting a divorce. Expect to hear from my lawyer."

The condo was in my name. I had purchased it before we were married, and since I had never added his name to the deed, he had no rights to it. There was no question he would be the one leaving.

My husband just stared at me with his jaw hanging open like he couldn't believe it. "But Jennifer," he whined. "You don't understand. Let me explain."

"There's nothing to understand," I told him sadly. "This is a deal breaker for me, and you know that as well as I do. We are done."

The girl had taken his hand and smiled triumphantly. "Come on baby," she told him. "Zip up and let's get out of here. We can finally be together like we planned."

"Yeah baby," I had sneered. "I'll box up your stuff. It'll be in the hallway tomorrow. Pick it up by six o'clock or I'm trashing it all."

After they left my first call was to the locksmith, but my second call was to Susan.

That night was the last time I had seen my husband until we had met for the court-ordered pre-divorce mediation. He spent most of that session reiterating what he had told me in numerous voice mails, emails and sessions spent yelling on the other side of my front door. He loved me. He had made a terrible mistake. He wasn't going to sign the papers. We were meant to be together. Needless to say, mediation hadn't been very successful. Fortunately, I had been careful to keep our assets separate, as if I knew that someday I would be in this situation.

Through it all, Susan had been my rock. In the end I don't think I was even that sad about the divorce, I was really angrier with myself for staying in a relationship that wasn't fulfilling with a man I didn't love anymore.

"You need to get some quality sex." Susan drew my attention back to the present. "Bang him out of your system."

"I don't know," I answered slowly. "I think I need a hiatus."

"A hiatus from what?" Susan asked with a frown. "You haven't had sex in what, eighteen months?"

I nodded. "Yeah, but I just can't take a disappointing fumble right now. I would rather have nothing than another three-pump chump."

I shook my head and continued, "I'm going to stick with my battery-operated boyfriend, he never disappoints me."

Susan smiled. "That's because you know your way around your own vajayjay."

She motioned to the waiter to bring us a third bottle of wine.

"That's why I like to date women," she continued. "We already know our way around the equipment."

I nodded thoughtfully. "You make a good point."

Susan leaned forward. "We've never talked about this," she said earnestly. "Have you ever been with a woman?"

For more of the story, check out "The Divorcee's First Time" by Reba Bale, available for immediate download[1] today.

***

Want a free book? Join my newsletter and a special gift. I'll contact you a few times a month with story updates, new releases, and special sales. Visit bit.ly/RebaBaleSapphic[2] for more information.

---

1. **https://books2read.com/u/bpznKX**

2. https://bit.ly/RebaBaleSapphic

Other Books by Reba Bale

Check out my other books, available on most major online retailers now. Go to my webpage[1] at bit.ly/AuthorRebaBale to learn more.

Friends to Lovers Lesbian Romance Series

The Divorcee's First Time
My BFF's Sister
My Rockstar Assistant
My College Crush
My Fake Girlfriend
My Secret Crush
My Holiday Love
My Valentine's Gift
My Spring Fling
My Forbidden Love
Coming Out in Ten Dates
Worth Waiting For
My Office Wife
My Second Chance
My Party Planner
My Broken Heart

The Surrender Club Lesbian Romance Series

Jaded
Hated
Fated
Saved
Caged

The Sapphic Security Series

Guarding the Senator's Daughter

The Second Chances Series

1. https://books2read.com/ap/nB2qJv/Reba-Bale

Last Christmas

Menage Romances

Pie Promises

Tornado Warning

Summer in Paradise

Life of the Mardi

Bases Loaded

Two for One Deal

The Unexpectedly Mine Series

Sinful Desires

Taken by Surprise

Just One Night

Forbidden Desires

Love Is in the Air Series

Spanking & Sprinkles

Hotwife Erotic Romances

Hotwife in the Woods

Hotwife on the Beach

Hotwife Under the Tree

A Hotwife's Retreat

Hot Wife Happy Life

Want a free book? Just join my newsletter at bit.ly/RebaBaleSapphic[2]. ***You'll be the first to hear about new releases, special sales, and free offers.***

2. https://bit.ly/RebaBaleSapphic

About the Author

Reba Bale writes erotic romance, lesbian romance, menage romance, & the spicy stories you want to read on a cold winter's night. When Reba is not writing she is reading the same naughty stories she likes to write.

You can also follow Reba on Medium[3] for free stories, bonus epilogues and more. You can also hear all about new releases and special sales by joining Reba's newsletter mailing list.[4]

3. https://medium.com/@authorrebabale
4. https://bit.ly/rebabooks

Don't miss out!

Visit the website below and you can sign up to receive emails whenever Reba Bale publishes a new book. There's no charge and no obligation.

https://books2read.com/r/B-A-IDTM-ZSLTC

BOOKS 2 READ

Connecting independent readers to independent writers.

Printed in Great Britain
by Amazon